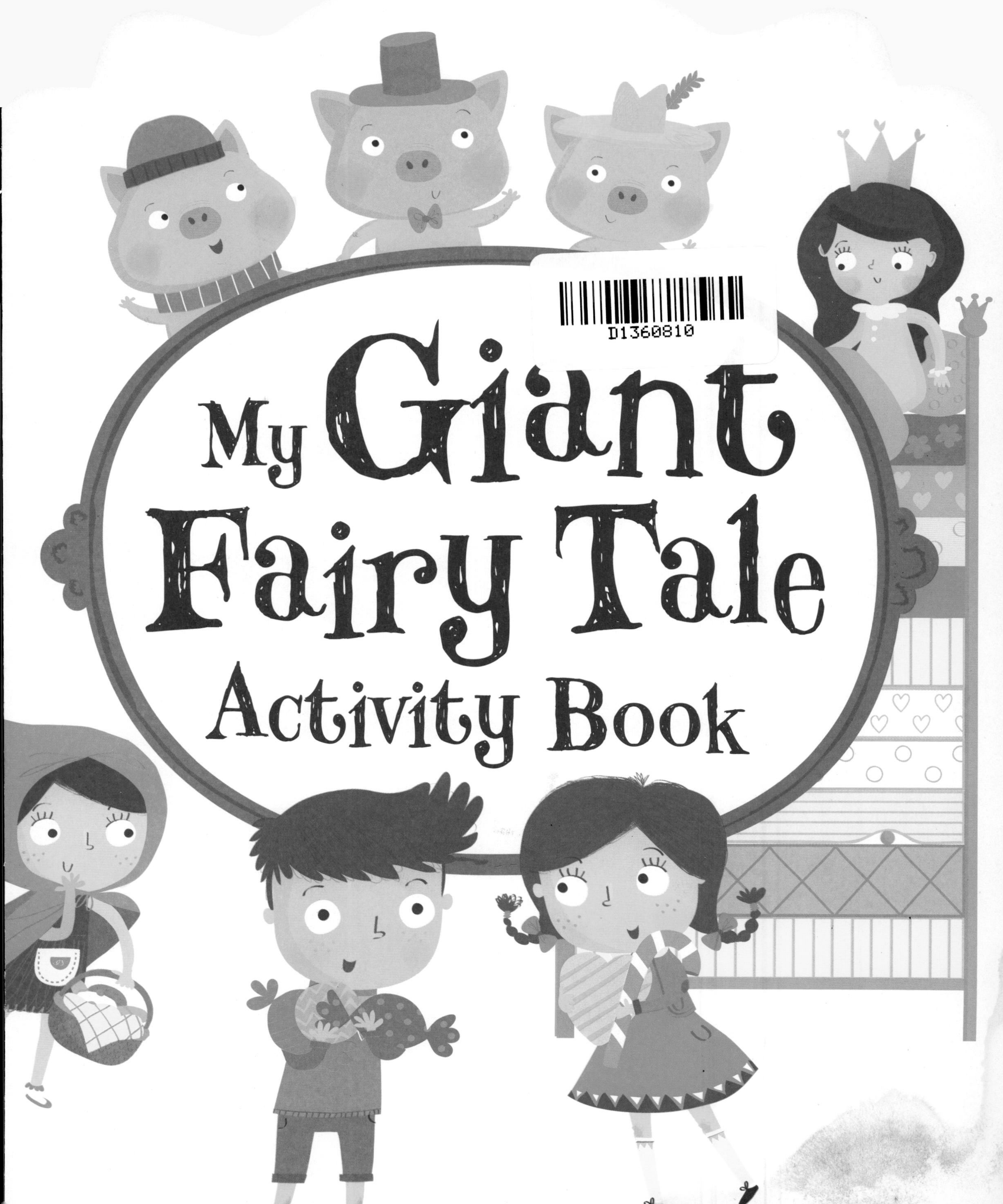

My Giant Fairy Tale Activity Book
D1360810

This edition published by Parragon Books Ltd in 2015 and distributed by

Parragon Inc.
440 Park Avenue South, 13th Floor
New York, NY 10016
www.parragon.com

Written by Cath Ard
The Three Little Pigs & Hansel and Gretel illustrated by Steve Wood
Little Red Riding Hood & The Princess and the Pea illustrated by Lauren Ellis and Amy Evans

ISBN 978-1-4748-0267-3

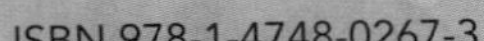

Printed in China

My Giant Fairy Tale Activity Book

Parragon

Bath • New York • Cologne • Melbourne • Delhi
Hong Kong • Shenzhen • Singapore • Amsterdam

Contents

The Three Little Pigs

The three little pigs

The big bad wolf

The friendly little rabbit

He is hidden somewhere on every double page. Can you find him?

Once upon a time, there were three little pigs who lived in a cozy house with their mommy.

One day, the three little pigs decided it was time they made their own way in the world. They each trotted off down a different path.

Answers: 1:C, 2:A, 3:B.

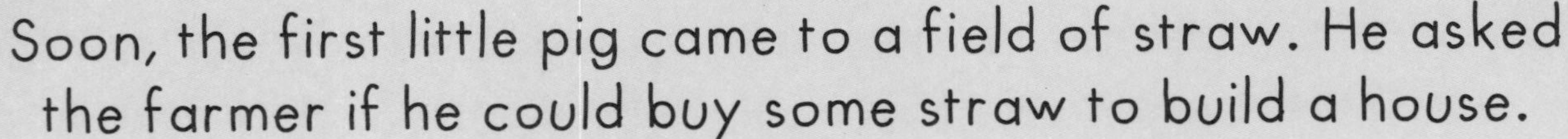

Soon, the first little pig came to a field of straw. He asked the farmer if he could buy some straw to build a house.

Check the box next to the farmer. He has blue overalls!

How many people have muddy boots? Color the number.

2 3 4

Answer: 3 people are wearing muddy boots.

The farmer agreed, so the little pig set about building his house.

By the evening, the house of straw was finished. The tired little pig went straight to bed.

Use the grid as a guide to copy the picture in the space below.

Color your picture!

Then there was a knock on the door.

Who is at the door?
Circle your answer.

wolf

squirrel

Little pig, little pig, let me come in.

Not by the hairs on my chinny-chin-chin!

E

D

B

A

C

Draw lines to match each shadow to a picture.

1 2 3 4 5

Answers: The wolf is at the door. 1:D, 2:C, 3:A, 4:E, 5:B.

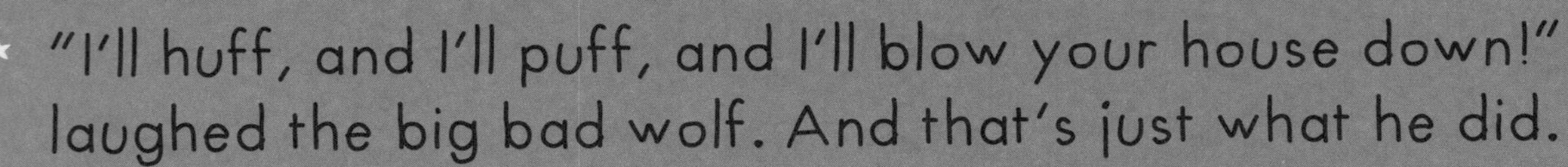

"I'll huff, and I'll puff, and I'll blow your house down!" laughed the big bad wolf. And that's just what he did.

Find and circle the things that are blowing away.

toothbrush

mug

teapot

teddy

clock

pan

Draw the little pig running away!

The little pig ran away as fast as
his little legs would carry him!
Help!
START
Draw a line to
the forest without
going off the road.
FINISH

In the forest, the second little pig met a woodcutter.
"Please may I buy some logs to build my house?" he asked.
Help yourself!
Draw a pile of logs in the little pig's cart.

How many acorns can you see? Color the number.

7 8 9

Can you find the big bad wolf?

Answer: There are 9 acorns.

The second little pig wanted to build his house near a bridge and next to an apple tree.

Draw a cross in the box where the little pig should build his house.

In no time at all, the little pig had built the wooden walls and roof.

The next morning, the second little pig woke up, brushed his teeth, and made breakfast. He was just about to eat, when he heard a loud knock on the door.

These four pictures have gotten mixed up. Number them in the order they happened.

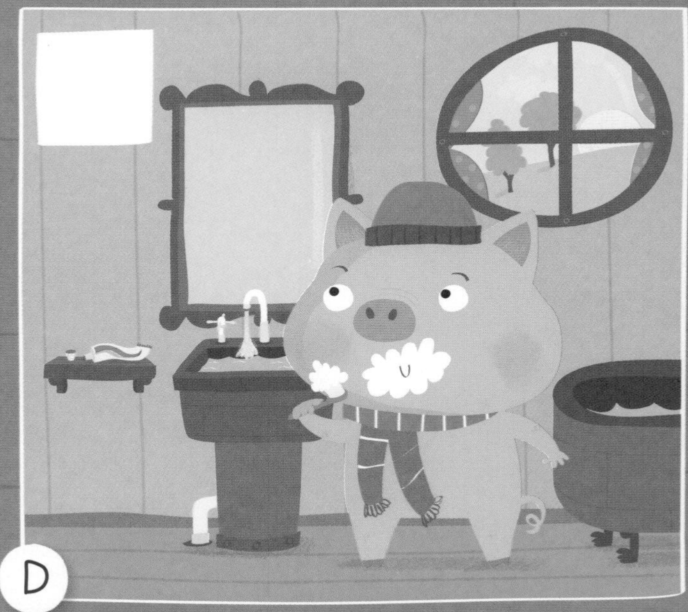

Answers: A:4, B:3, C:1, D:2.

"Little pig, little pig, let me come in," growled the wolf.
"Not by the hairs on my chinny-chin-chin!" squealed the little pig.

What did the wolf say next? Check the box.

Color the picture.

Answer: "Then I'll huff, and I'll puff, and I'll blow your house down!"

The third little pig had reached a busy building site.
He asked a builder if he could buy some bricks to build a house.

Check each of these as you find them.
This digger has dug up a dinosaur bone! Find and circle two more.

The third little pig went to buy some tools to build his house.

Help the little pig find the tools he needs. Check off each one on the shopping list.

All day long, the third little pig worked hard.
Draw the other half of the little pig's house.

The third little pig was hungry after all his hard work, so he set off to the market to buy some food.

Color the white roofs to complete each repeating pattern.

Count the market stalls and color the number.

6 7 8

Find and circle the naughty puppy.

Answer: There are 8 market stalls. Row 1 needs a pink roof. Row 2 needs a red roof.

The third little pig made soup with the vegetables he had bought. He scrubbed, peeled, and chopped, then he put them all in a big pot with some water.

At last, the little pig sat down to enjoy a rest.

The third little pig saw his brothers and ran outside. They were being chased by the big bad wolf!

Follow the road to the third little pig's house.

Don't get stuck behind ...

cars
carts
sheep
tractors

Help!

START

Which of these bridges do the little pigs cross on the way? Check the box.

Answer: The bridge without the sheep on it.

The third little pig quickly let his brothers in. The wolf banged on the front door and peeked through the mail slot.

Quick! Color the strong door to keep the wolf out.

Little pigs, little pigs, let me come in.

Not by the hairs on our chinny-chin-chins!

Find and circle the door key.

"Then I'll huff, and I'll puff, and I'll blow your house down!" cried the wolf. So he huffed and puffed ... and he huffed and puffed. But the brick house stood strong.

Find four differences between these two pictures.

Color in a picture of the wolf's head for each difference you find.

Answers: The bird is missing, the door is blue, the laundry basket is red, the red T-shirt is missing.

The big bad wolf was furious that he couldn't blow the house down! Then he had an idea ...

Color each shape to match the dot, and see the wolf's idea.

The big bad wolf climbed down the chimney. PLOP! He landed right in the pot of soup!

YEEOW!

Color the picture.

The wolf needs to cool off! Check where he should go.

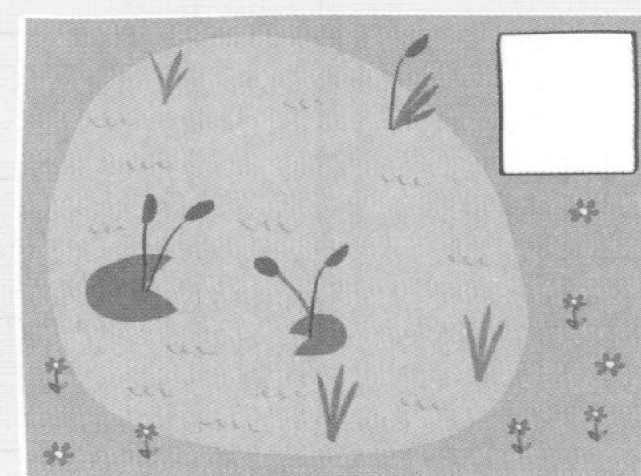

Answer: The wolf should go to the lake to cool off.

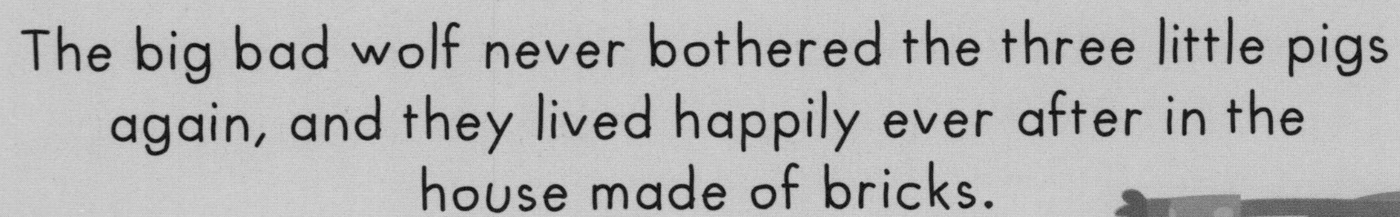

The big bad wolf never bothered the three little pigs again, and they lived happily ever after in the house made of bricks.

Draw the three little pigs eating their soup.

Draw family photos in the frames.

The Princess and the Pea

The Prince

Princess Jade

The King and Queen

The Prince's puppy

He is hidden somewhere on every double page. Can you find him?

Once upon a time, there was a lonely prince. He lived in a big castle with a pretty garden, but he wished he had someone special to share it with.

Draw a lovely princess for the Prince to dream about!
The Prince is holding one apple. Find four more.

The Queen did her best to help. She planned a grand ball at the palace. The royal messenger delivered invitations to all the palaces in nearby kingdoms.

Circle the palace the Queen forgot to send an invitation to!

Which palace would you like to live in?

Answers: 1:C, 2:D, 3:E, 4:A. The queen forgot palace B.

On the night of the ball, the grand hall was filled with excited princesses.

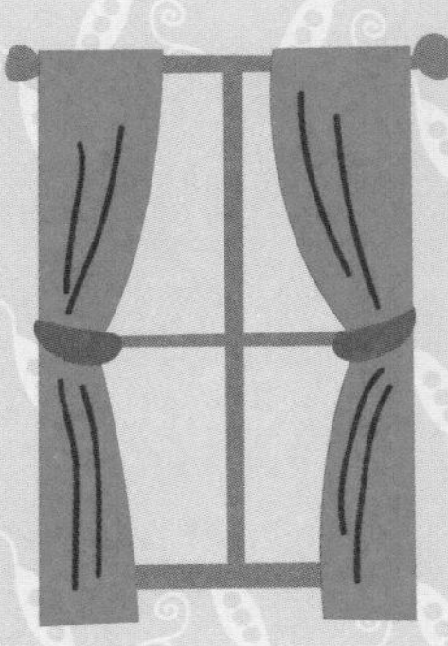

But none of these princesses are quite right!

Doodle more princesses dancing to the music.

Find and circle ...
a tall princess
a small princess
a pink princess
a sleepy princess
Tee-hee!
Three princesses have
forgotten their crowns!
Draw them each a tiara.

After a while, the King and Queen ran out of princesses for the Prince to meet. So he saddled his horse, waved goodbye, and set off to find a bride.

Help the Prince find a safe route through the kingdom.

Don't go past ...
creepy caves
sleeping bears
fire-breathing dragons

Start

How many rabbits does the Prince pass along the way? Color the number.

1 2 3

Answer: The Prince passes 3 rabbits.

The Prince traveled far and wide. Along the way, he met lots of talented princesses. Princess Grace loved to dance, Princess Amelia loved to bake, and Princess Ellie loved to paint!

Draw lines to match each princess to her shadow.

1

2

3

A

B

C

How many princesses are wearing hearts? Color the number!

2 3

Dancing makes me dizzy!

Answers: 1:C, 2:A, 3:B. 2 princesses are wearing hearts.

Princess Alice loved kittens, Princess Sophie loved feathers, and Princess Violet loved flowers!

Which princess has made the Prince sneeze? Follow the ribbons to find out.

Answer: Princess Violet has made the Prince sneeze.

But in his heart, the Prince knew he had not met the princess of his dreams, so he took out his map and headed home.

Draw a map for the Prince to follow home.

When he got home, the Prince told the King and Queen how sad he was.

Color in the other half of the King and Queen!

That night, there was a terrible storm. Just as the royal family sat down to eat their dinner, there was a loud RAT-A-TAT-TAT at the castle door.

The royal dinner is the best in the land! check off the three things you think the Prince should eat tonight.

The Prince opened the door to find a very wet girl outside.

Draw the Prince in the doorway.

My name is Princess Jade.

Add ducks and frogs splashing in the puddles.

The girl didn't look much like a princess, but princes must always be polite, so he invited her inside.

Circle the things that Princess Jade will need to get warm and dry.

Sweater

Fan

Hot-water bottle

Towels

Swimsuit

Answer: She will need the sweater, hot-water bottle, and towels.

When the Princess had warmed up, the maid brought some dry clothes for her.

Answer: The two red shoes make a pair.

All evening long, the Prince and the Princess talked and laughed. By bedtime, the Prince had fallen in love!

These four pictures have gotten mixed up! Number them in the order that they happened.

Answers: A:4, B:1, C:3, D:2.

The Queen was delighted, but she wanted to be sure that Princess Jade was a *real* princess. She made a plan to find out.

The Queen needs something small and round. Which of these should she choose?

Draw a line between the two items that are exactly the same.

Answers: The Queen should choose the pea! The diamonds are exactly the same.

The Queen chose a tiny pea. She put it under the mattress, then she told the maids to pile the bed high with all the mattresses and blankets they could find.

Color the white blankets to complete each repeating pattern.

Answer: Row 1 needs a pink blanket. Row 2 needs a green blanket. Row 3 needs a blue blanket.

When the Queen showed Princess Jade to her bedroom, the girl gazed up at the towering bed in surprise.

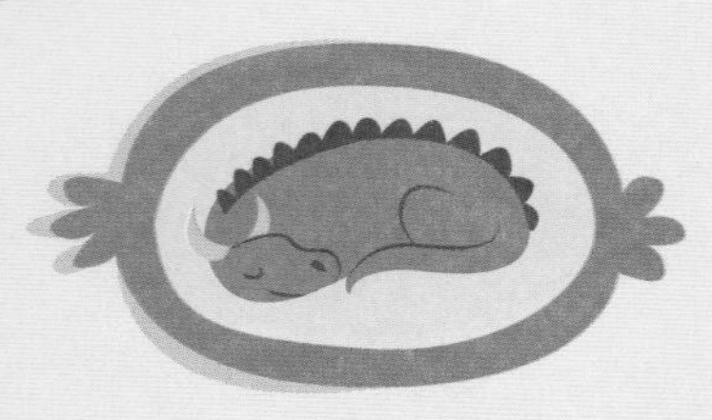

Help the Princess to count the mattresses as she climbs into bed. Add the missing numbers.

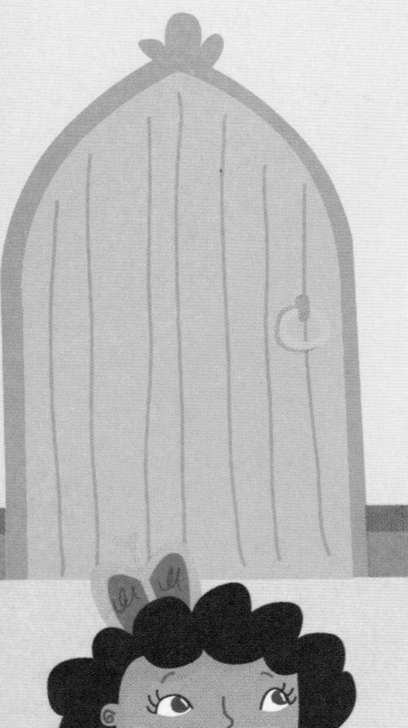

Up I go!
One ... two ...

Color in all of the mattresses!

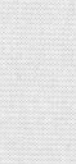

Answer: The missing numbers are 2, 4, 5, 7.

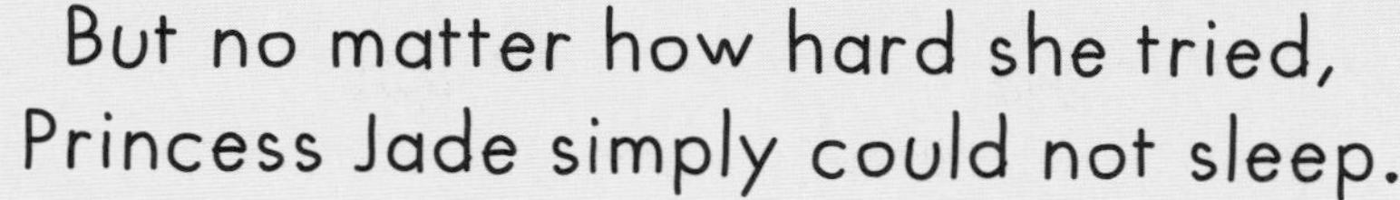

But no matter how hard she tried,
Princess Jade simply could not sleep.

What is Princess Jade thinking about to help her sleep? Color the shapes with a dot to see!

"Did you sleep well?" the Queen asked the next day. "I'm afraid not," said the Princess sleepily. "There was something in my bed, and it kept me awake all night!"

Draw crowns for each of the royal family.

How many silver spoons can you see? Color the number.

3 4 5

Answer: There are 5 silver spoons.

"So you *are* a real princess!" cried the Queen.
"Will you marry me, Princess Jade?" asked the Prince.
"Yes, I will!" cried Princess Jade.

Can you find five differences between these two pictures?

Color a crown for each difference that you find.

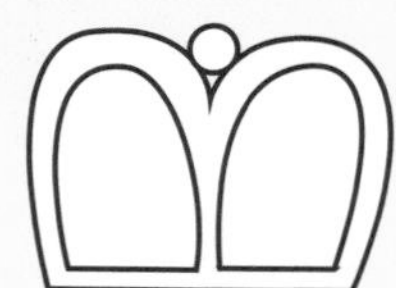

Answer: The pitcher is blue, mouse is missing, water is orange, king's plate is missing, bacon is upside down.

The Prince and Princess were married the very next day!

Draw the Prince, Princess, and bridesmaids at the wedding.

Find and circle the person with the tallest hat.

Oops!

Wait for us!

People came from all over
the kingdom to celebrate.
Color in the party!

Find and circle ...

And they all lived happily ever after!

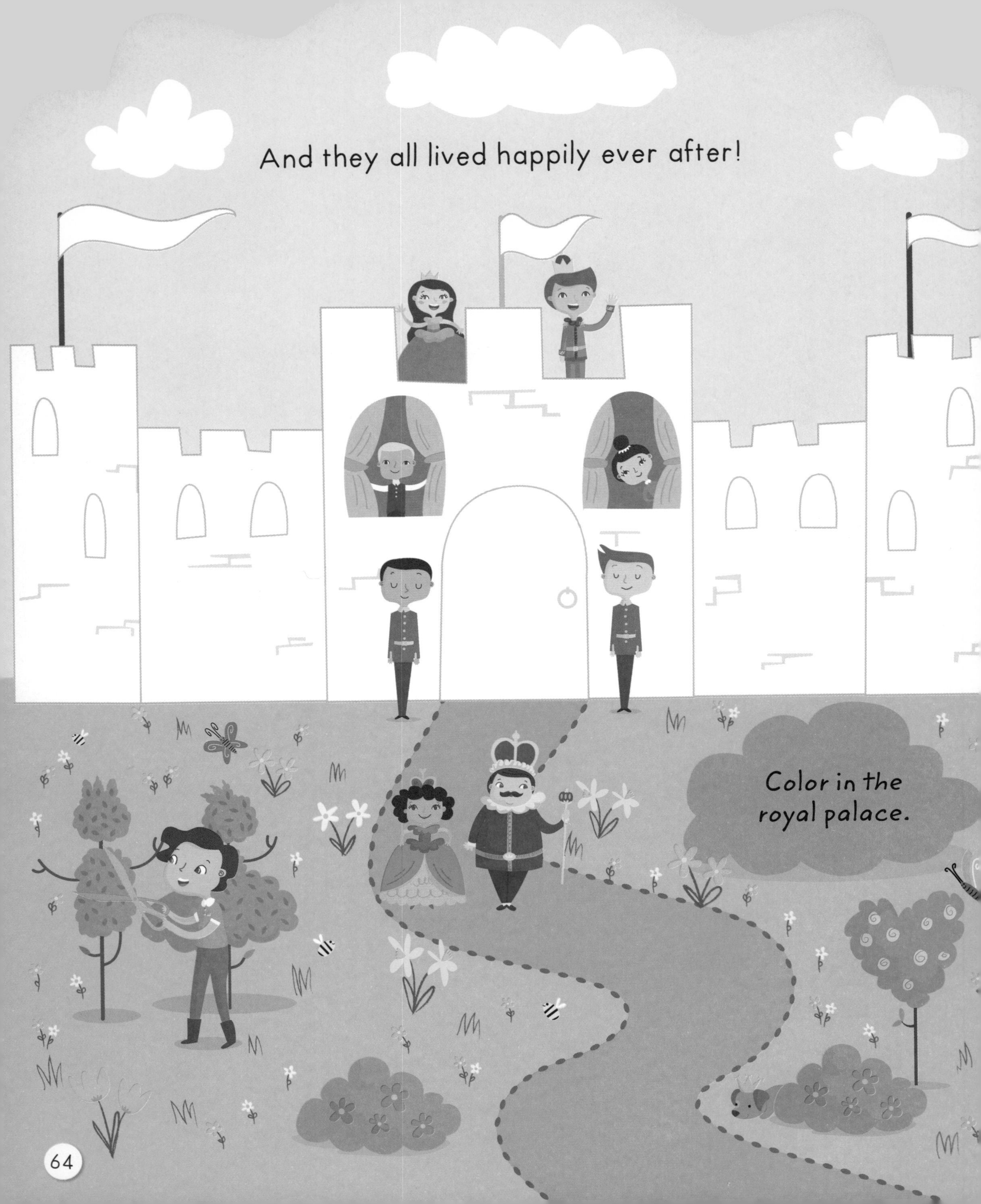

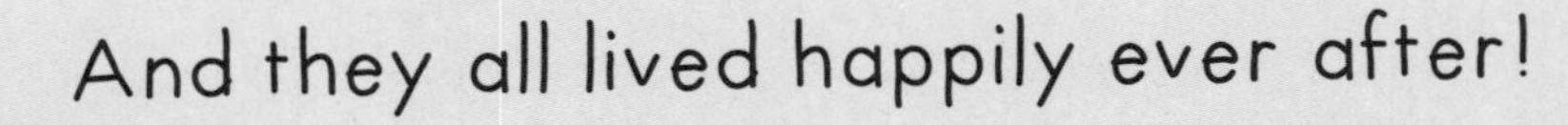

Color in the royal palace.

Hansel and Gretel

Hansel and Gretel

The witch

The little mouse

He is hidden somewhere on every double page. Can you find him?

Hansel and Gretel lived by a big forest with their father and mean old aunt. They were very poor.

Gretel has lost her rag doll. Can you find it?

How many spiders can you see? Color the number.

3 4 5

Answer: There are 5 spiders.

One night, the children overheard their aunt talking. "We have too many mouths to feed," she told their father.

The next morning, their aunt led them into the forest. But clever Hansel dropped a trail of breadcrumbs, so that they would be able to find their way home.

Can you see a squirrel hiding near the path?
Draw Hansel and Gretel at the end of the breadcrumb trail.

When they were deep in the forest, their aunt
told the children to wait while she went to chop wood.
Wait here until it gets dark.
Let's find some sticks for a fire!
Look at all these animals!
Hansel has gathered three sticks. Find and circle five more.
Can you find these animals?
Check the box as you find each one.
an animal with a white tail
an animal with an orange tail
an animal with a gray tail

Draw more animals in the clearing.

Hansel and Gretel soon fell asleep. When they woke up, it was dark and the little fire had gone out.

TWIT-TWOO!

Fill the night sky with stars and the forest with animals.

When morning came, Hansel and Gretel looked for the trail of breadcrumbs. But the birds had eaten them!
Circle the bird with red feathers and a yellow beak.
Draw a bird gobbling up the last crumbs!

Then one of the birds flew into the forest.
The children decided to follow it.

Draw a line to follow the bird without going off the path.

Check the nest the children pass.

Answer: They pass the green nest with blue eggs.

At the end of the path, Hansel and Gretel came upon a house made of gingerbread. Even the garden was filled with candy and sweets!

Color the house
and decorate it with
more candies!
Add four gingerbread men
to finish the fence.

The hungry children began to feast on the candy!

Can you find five differences between these two pictures?

Color in a candy for each difference that you find!

Answer: Chocolate missing from tree, bite out of roof, bite out of window, candy cane missing, squirrel has eaten candy.

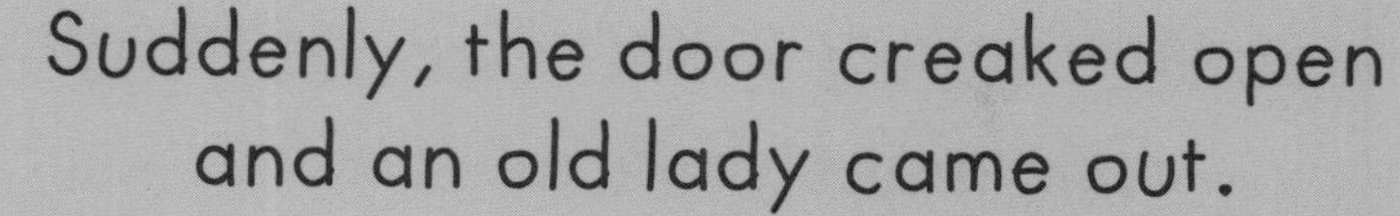

Suddenly, the door creaked open
and an old lady came out.

What do you think the old lady looks like? Draw her in the doorway.

Now color in the candies on the house!

The old woman invited Hansel and Gretel inside. She brought out dish after dish piled high with delicious food. The children ate until they were ready to burst!

How many pancakes have flipped out of the pan? Color the number.

3 4 5

18 Answers: 3 pancakes have flipped out of the pan. Shadow A matches the cake perfectly.

The old woman showed the children to a room with two soft beds. They snuggled down under the blankets and fell fast asleep.

Use the grid as a guide to copy the picture below.

Now color your picture!

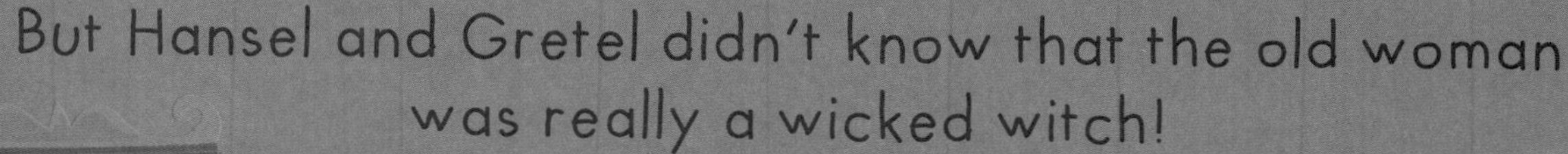

But Hansel and Gretel didn't know that the old woman was really a wicked witch!

Tee-hee-hee! I'll fatten them up, then these children will make a nice meal for ME!

What clues can you find that show the old woman is really a witch?

Answer: Any of: broomstick, witch's hat, witch's dress and shoes, potion bottle, spell book.

The next morning, the witch dragged Hansel
from his bed and locked him in a big cage!
Draw poor Hansel
trapped in the cage!
I'll soon fatten
you up for
my dinner!
Find one bat, then
draw three more!

She told Gretel to cook a
big breakfast for her brother.

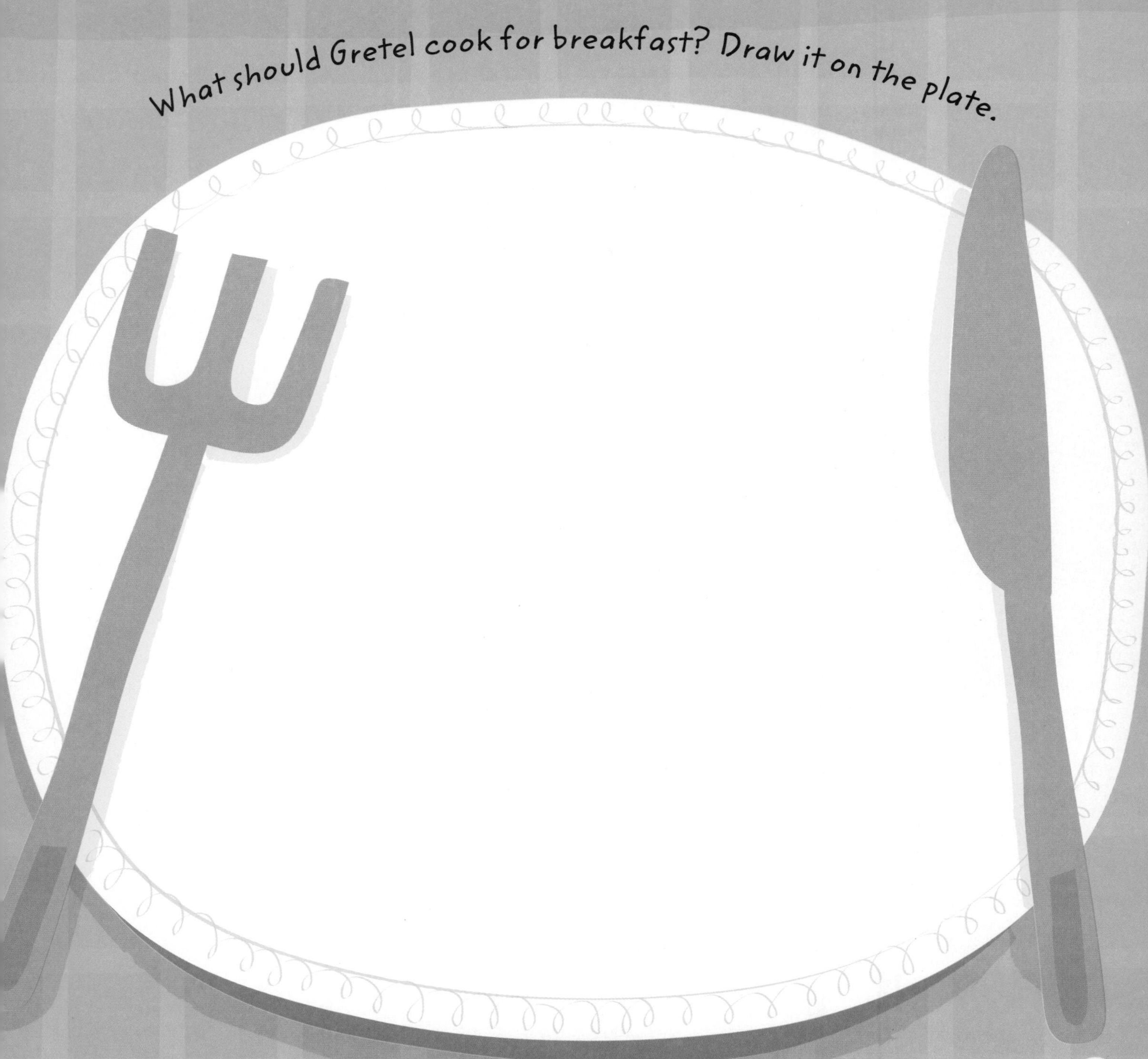

Gretel had to cook, carry, fetch, and clean all day long, while the witch waited for Hansel to grow fat enough to eat.

Which five things will Gretel need to clean the house? Circle each one.

Answer: She needs the broom, mop, pail, dustpan, and vacuum cleaner.

Each day, the witch made Hansel hold out his finger to feel if he was getting fatter. But Hansel knew the old witch could hardly see, so he held out something thin to trick her.

Draw lines to match the pairs of food. The only thing without a pair is the one Hansel chooses!

Still too scrawny!

What did Hansel choose? Draw a line between it and his hand.

Answer: Hansel chose the chicken leg.

Finally, the witch grew tired of waiting. She ordered Gretel to fetch some logs from the bottom of the garden.

Which trail of footprints leads Gretel to the logs?

How many creatures are on the log pile? Color the number.

4 5 6

Answers: The light green footprints lead to the log pile. There are 4 creatures.

"Whether he be fatter or thinner, I'll have Hansel for my dinner!" the witch sang as she lit the oven.

Color the picture below to match.

The witch ordered Gretel to crawl into the oven.
She was going to eat Gretel, too!
But clever Gretel had a plan.

Gretel pushed the witch into the oven!
Now she needed to find the key and unlock Hansel's cage.

Gretel knows the key is in a spotted tin.
Circle the tin to help her find it!

Answer: There are 2 green books.

When Gretel had freed Hansel, the children began to explore the house. Before long, they discovered an attic full of gold and jewels!

Find and circle ...
Wow!
Give Hansel and Gretel a crown each.

The children set off into the forest to find their way home.

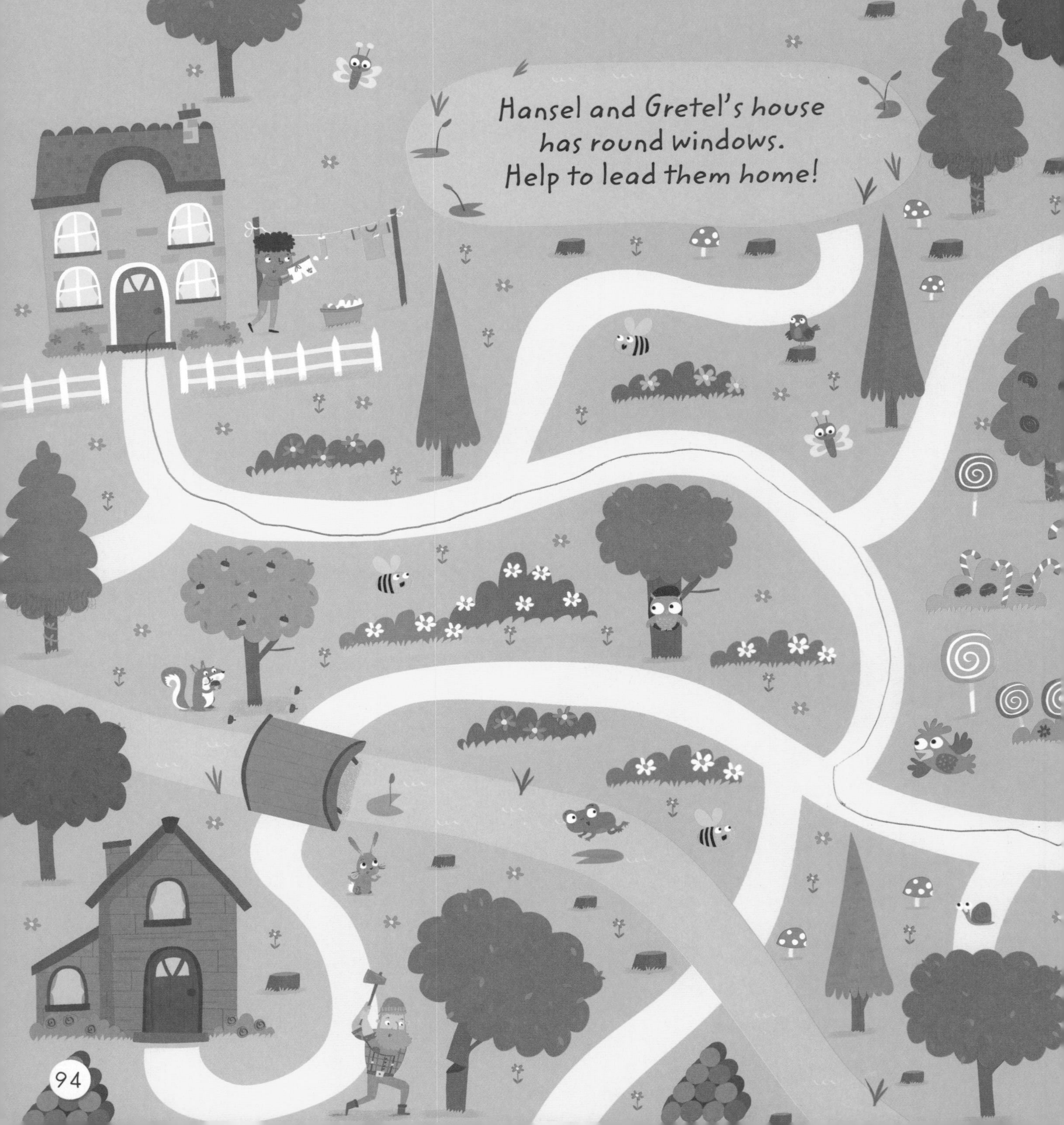

Hansel and Gretel's house has round windows. Help to lead them home!

Check the bridge
they cross on the way.
Answer: They cross the bridge with a handrail.

At home, they discovered that their mean aunt had left. Hansel and Gretel lived happily ever after with their father.

Little Red Riding Hood

Little Red Riding Hood, Mommy and Grandma

The wolf

Little Red Riding Hood's kitten

She is hidden somewhere on every double page. Can you find her?

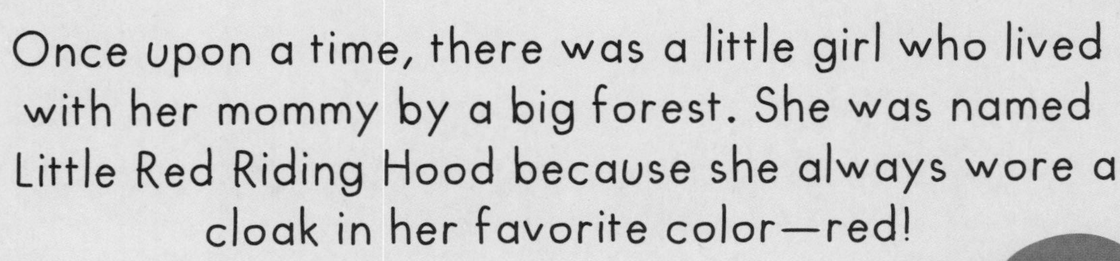

Once upon a time, there was a little girl who lived with her mommy by a big forest. She was named Little Red Riding Hood because she always wore a cloak in her favorite color—red!

Doodle some red toys for Little Red Riding Hood.

Count three red apples.
Draw two more.
Color the door in Little Red Riding Hood's
favorite color. Draw some curtains, too!

One day, a delicious smell of baking filled the cottage. Grandma was feeling unwell, and Mommy was cooking for her.

Draw a picture of Mommy and Little Red Riding Hood.
I'll take Grandma a basket of yummy food.

Grandma lived on the other side of the forest, so Mommy helped Little Red Riding Hood draw a map.

Can you help, too?

"Now hurry along," said Mommy. "And remember, don't talk to any strangers along the way."

Color the picture below to match.

Little Red Riding Hood waved goodbye to
Mommy and set off for Grandma's house.
START
Grandma's house has a blue door.
Follow the path to help Little Red
Riding Hood find it.

Circle
the wolf!

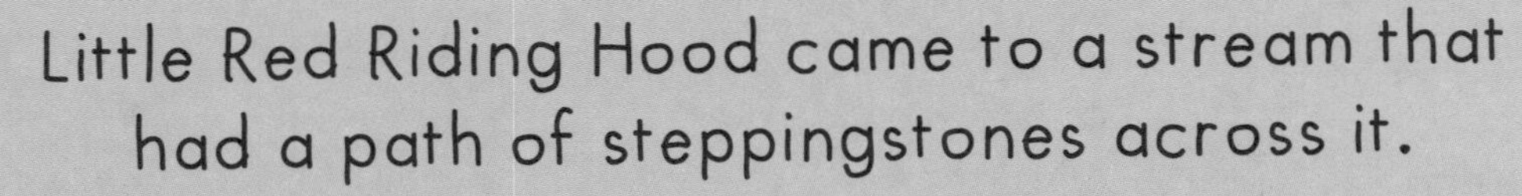

Little Red Riding Hood came to a stream that had a path of steppingstones across it.

Count the steppingstones and color the number.

3

4

5

I hope I don't get my feet wet!

Circle all the ducks!

Answer: There are 5 steppingstones.

Doodle a frog on each empty lily pad.
Circle the tadpole that is the odd one out.
1
2
3
4
5
6
7
8
Answer: Tadpole 5 is the odd one out.

On the other side of the stream were some butterflies fluttering around beautiful flowers.

Suddenly, Little Red Riding Hood heard a growly voice. She jumped with surprise!

Who is talking to Little Red Riding Hood? Check the box.

rabbit ☐ wolf ☐

Point to the parts of the wolf!

big eyes
sharp claws
furry tail
big ears
big teeth

Answer: The wolf is talking to Little Red Riding Hood.

"I'm going to visit Grandma," said Little Red Riding Hood.
"How kind," said the wolf, licking his lips greedily.
Grandma sounded like a tasty treat to eat!

Draw the wolf running to Grandma's house.

Answer: The red paw prints lead the wolf to Grandma's house.

The hungry wolf crept inside Grandma's house. He dashed into the bedroom and gobbled up Grandma in one GULP!

Can you find five differences between these two pictures?

Color a ball of yarn for each difference that you find.

Answers: The wolf has a big belly, the picture on the left has fallen off the wall, Grandma is missing, Red Riding Hood's eyes are closed in the picture on the right, the basket of yarn has been knocked over.

The wolf put on Grandma's glasses and took a nightcap and nightgown from the closet.

Dress the wolf in Grandma's nightcap and nightgown by coloring them in.

shoes ☐ slippers 

Which pair should the wolf put on? Check the box.

Answer: The wolf should put the slippers on.

The wolf waited for Little Red Riding Hood. He closed the curtains, clambered into bed, and pulled the quilt up to his chin.

Color each shape on the quilt to match the dot in the middle.

Draw a picture of Grandma here.
Count the balls of yarn, and color the number.
7 8 9
Which of these could Grandma knit with her yarn? Check the box.
scarf
boot

When Little Red Riding Hood reached Grandma's house, she found the front door wide open.

That's strange!
Why's Grandma's
door open?

Color
Grandma's house.

Little Red Riding Hood
went upstairs to Grandma's
bedroom.

Draw lines to match the pictures to the shadows.

1 

2 

3 

4 

5 

Are you in bed, Grandma?

Yes, my dear. Come closer.

C

D

E

Answers: 1:B, 2:D, 3:A, 4:E, 5:C.

Little Red Riding Hood gasped. Grandma looked so ... different. First, she saw the ears. Then she saw the eyes. Then she saw the teeth!

These four pictures have gotten mixed up! Number them in the order they happened.

Answers: A:3, B:1, C:4, D:2.

Little Red Riding Hood screamed and ran away, but the wolf chased her around Grandma's house.

The wolf was too quick! He gobbled Little Red Riding Hood up in a single GULP!

The greedy wolf is full! Draw a line to connect the two pictures of him that are exactly the same.

Answer: 1 and 6 are exactly the same.

Then the wolf howled happily.

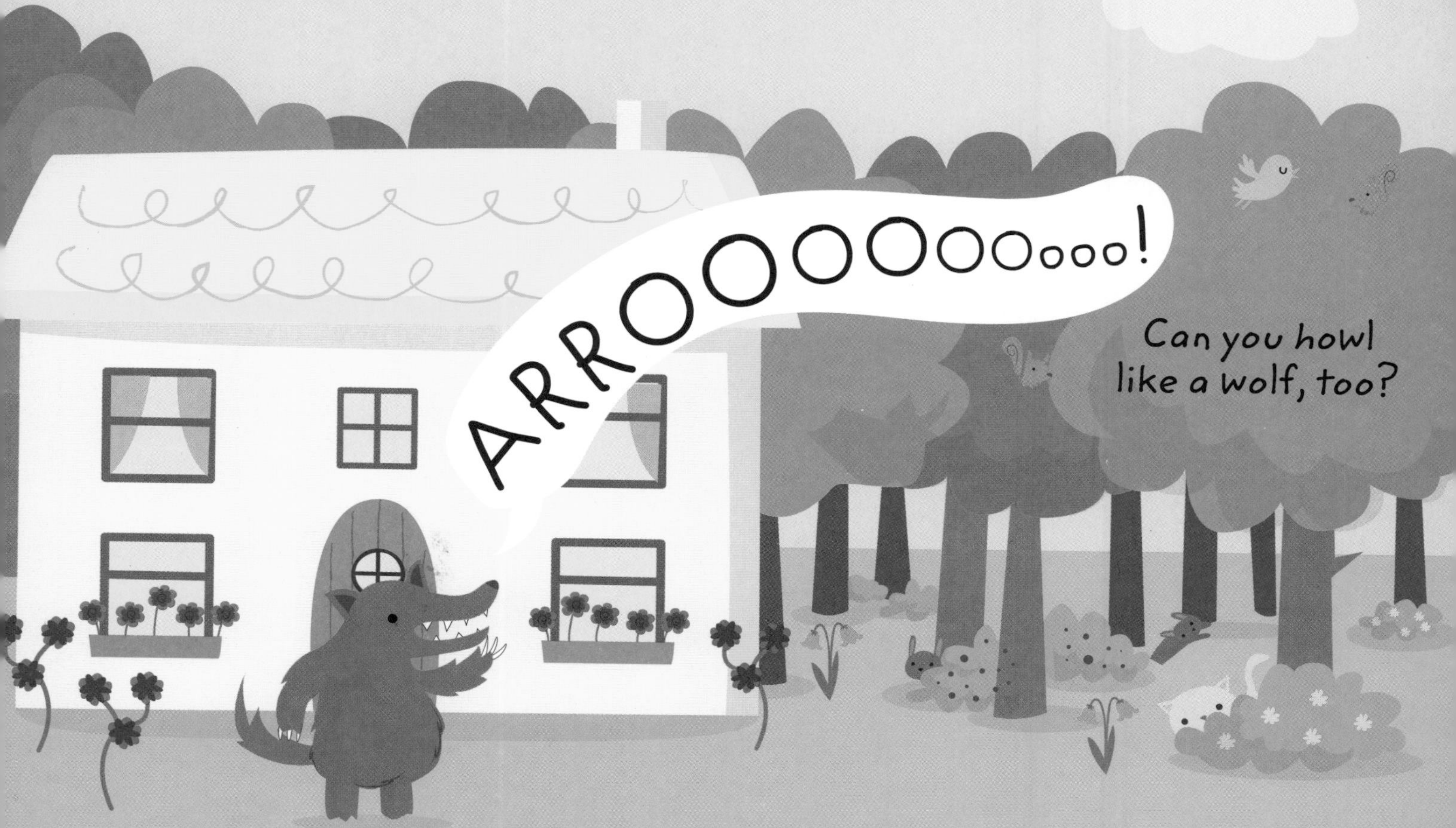

ARROOOOOOooo!

Can you howl like a wolf, too?

Draw a line to match each animal to the sound it makes.

Answers: 1:C, 2:A, 3:D, 4:B.

Nearby, a woodcutter heard the wolf's howl.

When the woodcutter saw the wolf's big belly, he picked him up and shook him! Out tumbled Grandma and Little Red Riding Hood.

Color the picture.

The wolf ran away into the forest, and he was never seen again.
Where will he go?
Follow the trail of paw prints to see where the wolf goes.
Find and circle ...